Waiting for Christmas

BY MONICA GREENFIELD

ILLUSTRATED BY JAN SPIVEY GILCHRIST

SCHOLASTIC PRESS · New York

For my daughter, Kamaria—You are my most precious gift.
M. G.

For Marietta Morrell, Yvette, Femi, and Teri Lewis,
for the love and family you gave me.
J. S. G.

Library of Congress Cataloging-in-Publication Data
Greenfield, Monica. Waiting for Christmas / by Monica Greenfield;
illustrated by Jan Spivey Gilchrist. p. cm.
Summary: Highlights various activities done in anticipation
of Christmas. ISBN 0-590-52700-2
[1. Christmas—Fiction.]
I. Gilchrist, Jan Spivey, ill. II. Title.
PZ7.G8456Wai 1996
[E]—dc20   95-35945 CIP AC
12 11 10 9 8 7 6 5 4 3 2 1   6 7 8 9/9 0 1/0
Printed in the U.S.A.   36
First printing, October 1996 The paintings are acrylic on
rag content paper. The text type was set in Cloister by
WLCR New York.

Thanks to my models, Sage Alexandra Mahoney and
Breck Ian Mahoney; and to Mrs. Gwendolyn Watts, for
the use of her beautiful house. J. S. G.

We slide outside down a snowy hill,

We warm our bodies by the fireplace,

We drink hot cider with cinnamon sticks,

We decorate and wait for Christmas.

We look for our presents one more time,

We give good-night kisses and head for bed,

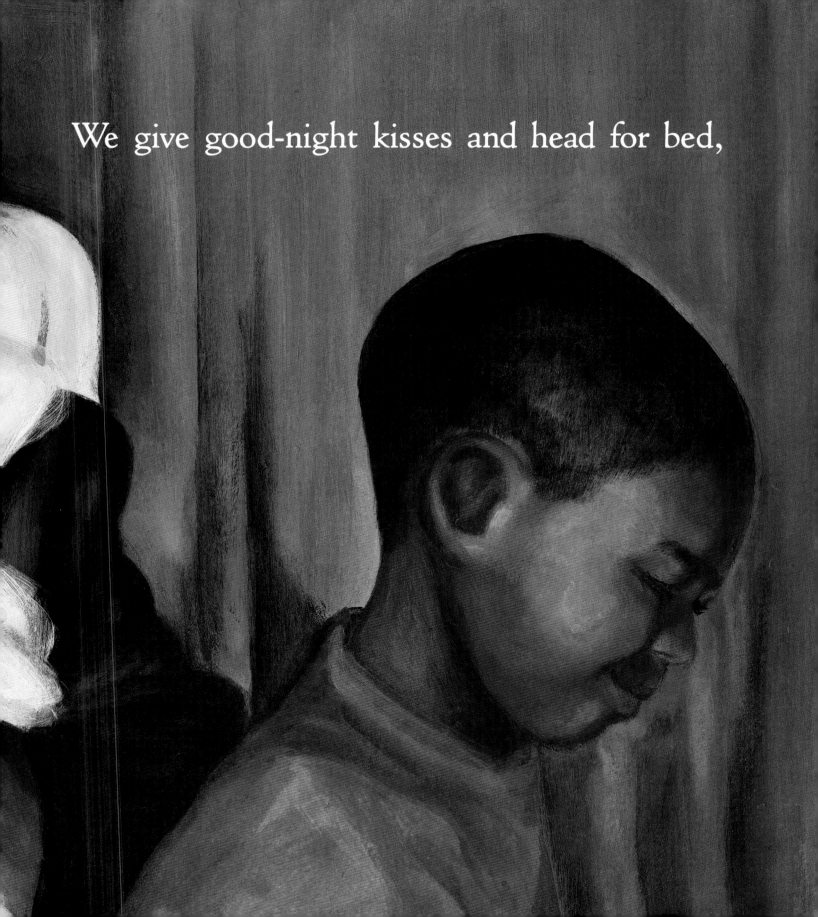

We really don't want to but it's getting late,

We just can't wait for Christmas.

We smile as the sunlight hits our lids,

We know the moment has finally come,

We fly downstairs to meet the day,

At last it's time to say . . .

Merry
Christmas!

Waiting for Christmas

BY MONICA GREENFIELD

We slide outside down a snowy hill,
We warm our bodies by the fireplace,
We drink hot cider with cinnamon sticks,
We decorate and wait for Christmas.

We look for our presents one more time,
We give good-night kisses and head for bed,
We really don't want to but it's getting late,
We just can't wait for Christmas.

We smile as the sunlight hits our lids,
We know the moment has finally come,
We fly downstairs to meet the day,
At last it's time to say . . .
Merry Christmas!